American edition published in 2013 by Andersen Press USA
an imprint of Andersen Press Ltd.
www.andersenpressusa.com

First published in Great Britain in 2013 by Andersen Press Ltd. 20 Vauxhall Bridge Road, London SW1V 2SA.
Published in Australia by Random House Australia Pty. Level 3, 100 Pacific Highway, North Sydney, NSW 2060.

Text copyright © Peter Bently, 2013. Illustration copyright © Mei Matsuoka, 2013.

Distributed in the United States and Canada by
Lerner Publishing Group, Inc.
241 First Avenue North
Minneapolis, MN 55401 USA

For reading levels and more information, look up this title at www.lernerbooks.com.

Color separated in Switzerland by Photolitho AG, Zürich. Printed and bound in Malaysia by Tien Wah Press.

Library of Congress Cataloging-in-Publication data available.
ISBN: 978-1-4677-3449-3   eBook ISBN: 978-1-4677-3454-7

1 - TWP - 12/1/13

To Lucy,
for the cosmic inspiration.
P. B.

To Uncle Peter,
for encouraging me to
reach great heights.
M. M.

The Great Balloon Hullaballoo

Peter Bently & Mei Matsuoka

ANDERSEN PRESS USA

Simon the Squirrel
was off to play ball,
But there stood
his mom with a
list in the hall.

"Please pop to the shop, Simon dearest. Here's money
For TP, new pants for yourself, bread and honey.

And one thing that's much
more important than these,
Tonight we've got pizza,
so don't forget CHEESE!"

So off trotted Simon with Rodney Raccoon.
Suddenly Simon said, "Look, it's the Moon!
Everybody knows that it's made out of cheese.
If we jump we can take just as much as we please!"

They ran to the lake in a mad gleeful dash,
Leapt from a tree trunk and landed—

KER-SPLASH!

"You pair of daft noodles! The Moon's in the sky!"
Laughed Bethany Bear, who stood
watching nearby.

"No problem!" said Simon. "We'll FLY to the Moon—

In Old Uncle
Somerset's
Special balloon!"

"You're all very welcome to go for a ride,"
Said Old Uncle Somerset. "Clamber inside!
Grab a nice cushion. There's plenty to try."
Then he untied the rope and they rose in the sky!

They shot into space with spectacular force

Until a great comet—

WHOOOOOSH!

—blew them off course!

"You've gone the wrong way!"
said a cow with a frown
(She had just jumped the Moon
and was on her way down.)

"Oh well," Simon said, as they sped through the stars,

"It looks like we'll have to go shopping on Mars!"

They landed on Mars and bought honey and bread

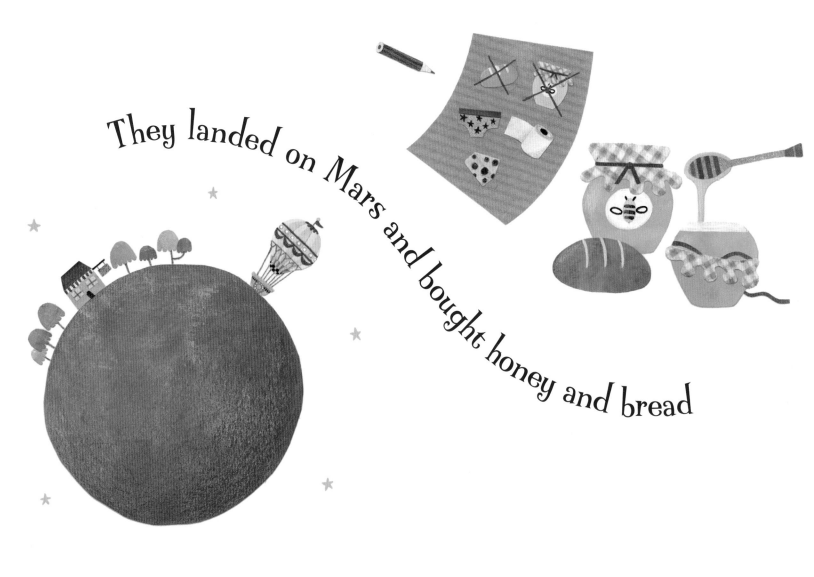

From a little green man with three eyes in each head.

Bethany called to her friends: "Look at me!

There's a wonderful view from this funny old tree.

But why is it covered in
hairy pink moss?"

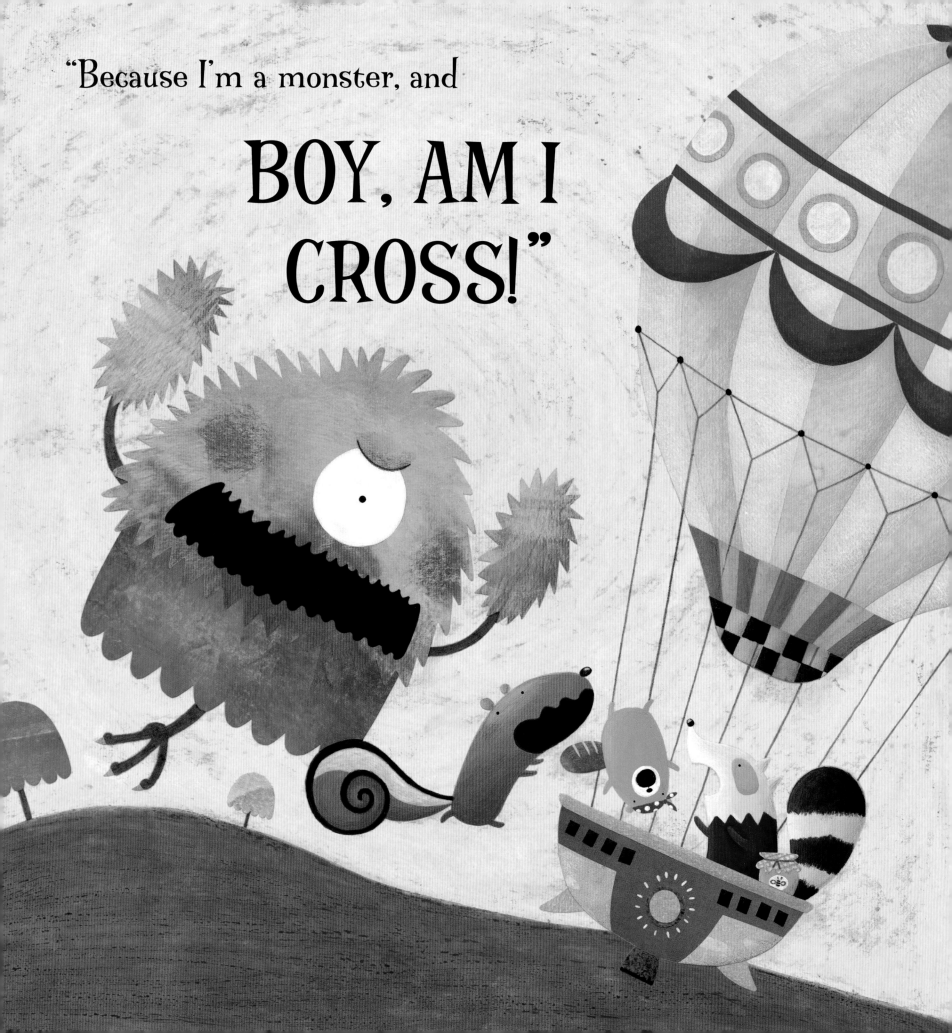

They fled from the monster and headed for Saturn,
Where Simon tried pants with a star-spangled pattern.

"Look at that weirdo!" the aliens said.
(On Saturn they all wear their pants on their head.)

At the store on Uranus, all shrouded in mist,
Simon said, "Toilet paper's next on Mom's list!"

"Of course!" grinned the Thing with the tentacled face,
"For TP this planet is just the right place!"

"Right," declared Simon. "Before we go back,
Why don't we stop for a drink and a snack?"

They called in at Pluto for cosmic rock cakes,

Which they ate at the Milky Way Parlor with shakes.

On Neptune
they hoped to get space
fish and fries.
Instead all they caught
was a scary surprise!
"Time to head home! Give it
maximum power!"
Said Simon,
then—

"Yikes! It's a meteor shower!"

Down poured the meteors. When would they stop?

Then—uh-oh!—they all heard a sound. It was

POP!

"Don't panic!" said Rodney. "It's under control!" And he climbed up and plonked his rear end on the hole.

They drifted back down to the earth with a

BUMP!

That made Uncle Somerset wake with a jump!

"Oh, don't mind the puncture,"
    he said. "I can patch it.
But you'd better run home to your mom
    or you'll catch it!"

Imagine the look of surprise on Mom's face
When Simon declared, "I've been shopping in space!"
"You can tell us about it at dinner time, please,"
Said his mom. "I've made pizzas. I just need the CHEESE."

Simon searched in the bag for the things on Mom's list.

"Whoops!" blushed the squirrel. "There's one thing I missed . . ."